Wedding Belles

by Alan Bailey
& Ronnie Claire Edwards

A SAMUEL FRENCH ACTING EDITION

SAMUEL FRENCH

FOUNDED 1830

NEW YORK HOLLYWOOD LONDON TORONTO

SAMUELFRENCH.COM

ISBN 978-0-573-69618-3   Printed in U.S.A.   #29030

IMPORTANT BILLING AND CREDIT REQUIREMENTS

All producers of *WEDDING BELLES must* give credit to the Author of the Play in all programs distributed in connection with performances of the Play, and in all instances in which the title of the Play appears for the purposes of advertising, publicizing or otherwise exploiting the Play and/or a production. The name of the Author *must* appear on a separate line on which no other name appears, immediately following the title and *must* appear in size of type not less than fifty percent of the size of the title type.

WEDDING BELLES was given its premiere in October, 2008 by One Thirty Productions in association with the City of Dallas' Office of Cultural Affairs and the Bath House Cultural Center. The production was directed by Larry Randolph. The cast was as follows:

BOBRITA TOLLIVER .... Sandra Looney

GLENDINE SLOCUMB .... Marty Van Kleeck

VIOLET MONTGOMERY .... Gene Raye Price

LAURA LEE MCINERNY ....Pam Myers-Morgan

IMA JEAN TATUM................................... Leslie Patrick

Larry Randolph designed the set, Marty Van Kleeck designed the costumes, Jason Moody designed the lighting, and M. Graeme Bice designed the sound.

CHARACTERS

LAURA LEE MCINERNY - 60
BOBRITA TOLLIVER - 60
VIOLET MONTGOMERY - 60
GLENDINE SLOCUMB - 60
IMA JEAN TATUM - 18

SETTING

The veranda and back garden of a large white house in Eufala Springs, an East Texas county seat with a population of three thousand. June, 1942.

ACT ONE

Scene 1

(The curtain rises. A hot June afternoon in Eufala Springs, Texas.)

(The back yard of a white two-story house with a wrap-around veranda. Overgrown planters and beds of flowers fill the yard. The home and grounds, once beautifully kept, are in disarray.)

(A screen door U.C. leads from the house onto the porch. Two large double windows flank the door. The L. window lets us see and hear the action inside the kitchen. In front of the R. window stands a desk and chintz-covered chair, the bottom falling out of it, a cushion on the seat to make it serviceable. Untidy stacks of magazines and news-papers tied with string fill the L. side of the porch.)

(Wide steps lead from the porch to the yard. A gate U.R. leads to the side yard. A trellis L. is covered with rambling roses. A white wicker table and chairs occupy a downstage corner.)

BOBRITA. *(calling from inside)* Laura Lee? – Hello? – Laura Lee? – Are you upstairs? –

*(**BOBRITA** comes out onto the porch. Early 60s, she is broad-shouldered and stout all over. A good old girl.)*

– Laura Lee? – Where are you? –

(She stops in her tracks when she sees the state of the yard.)

Oh, no – oh, no –

*(**GLENDINE** and **VIOLET** enter from the garden gate.)*

(**GLENDINE**, *a petite firecracker, wears a playsuit consisting of a cap-sleeved top and shorts with a skirt over them, unbuttoned down the front. Her ensemble is completed by espadrilles with ribbons tied around the ankles.*)

(**VIOLET** *is a little dumpling, roundish. She is frail, at least in her own mind.*)

GLENDINE. Laura Lee? –

VIOLET. – We're here! –

(*They, too, stop dead when they see the garden.*)

GLENDINE. Oh, no –

VIOLET. Oh, no –

(*They see* **BOBRITA** *on the porch.*)

GLENDINE. Where's Laura Lee?

BOBRITA. Not here.

(*The three women make their way from planter to planter, surveying the tangle.*)

GLENDINE. What in the world has she let happen to this garden?

BOBRITA. I wish you'd look. She's let her love-on-the-walk go completely to seed.

VIOLET. Poor things, these Sweet William are choking for water.

GLENDINE. You ought to see these hypatia.

(**BOBRITA** *and* **VIOLET**'s *paths cross.*)

BOBRITA. (*stiffly*) How are you getting along?

VIOLET. (*equally stiffly*) You needn't worry about me. I'm doing fine. I'm just living at the foot of the cross. It's level there.

BOBRITA. Well.

VIOLET. And I'm so much happier living in town instead of stranded out in the country. But I do miss the twins. How are they?

BOBRITA. Still frantic to enlist, but I'm fighting to keep them in school until they graduate.

GLENDINE. *(up on the porch)* Girls, you won't believe! This porch is a rat's nest.

VIOLET. What is all this junk stacked up?

BOBRITA. Looks like tin foil and scrap for the war effort.

GLENDINE. And all these papers.

VIOLET. Why hasn't she turned this in? They need these things.

GLENDINE. Where do you think she is?

BOBRITA. Any number of places. I talked to her this morning. She'd baked up a batch of cookies, took them down to the bus station for when the soldiers come through.

VIOLET. Was she set to do a Historical Home tour?

BOBRITA. Who knows? Her latest project she's taken on is to redo the Dewey Decimal system down at the library.

GLENDINE. You don't mean it.

VIOLET. Just keeping herself distracted, I guess.

GLENDINE. Poor thing.

BOBRITA. Too bad she's not tending to her own backyard.

GLENDINE. And she thinks she's going to host a Gala in a month's time?

BOBRITA. She'll never give up the Gala.

VIOLET. Not even after – ?

(She trails off.)

GLENDINE. – Oh! I had an idea last night, woke me up out of a deep sleep. I think what we could do for the Gala is put on a talent show. Plenty of people would buy tickets to that.

BOBRITA. But we don't have any talent.

GLENDINE. *(digging in)* I knew you'd shoot it down the very first thing –

BOBRITA. Not everybody likes to show off as much as you do, Glendine –

VIOLET. Wait, wait, don't say anything more! You can't do any Garden Club business until I get my minutes from the last meeting.

BOBRITA. *(impatiently)* Sister –

VIOLET. It won't take a second –

*(**VIOLET** hurries out the back gate to the car. As soon as she's off –)*

GLENDINE. *(desperately)* Bobrita, you've got to take her back. My marriage is at stake.

BOBRITA. When have you had a marriage that's not at stake?

GLENDINE. It's going on three weeks and she's driving Coach crazy.

BOBRITA. Tell me about it. Beaumont and I have had her underfoot for forty years.

GLENDINE. But she's your sister –

BOBRITA. She moved out on her own accord. We built her that perfectly nice little house. She refused to stay in it for even one night.

GLENDINE. Well, my nerves are raw. I don't think I can take another evening of sitting on the front porch 'til midnight playing Guess the Bible Verse –

*(**VIOLET** reappears with her notebook. **GLENDINE** quickly changes her tone.)*

(covering, brightly) – and Coach was so cute when he guessed that verse from Ruth: "Thy people shall be my people."

VIOLET. Wasn't that sweet? Just like I was family.

GLENDINE. *(weakly)* Just like you were family.

*(**BOBRITA**, then **GLENDINE**, start using this time to pull some weeds and straighten up the garden. **VIOLET** perches, not quite as eager to get to work.)*

VIOLET. *(to **BOBRITA**)* Speaking of family, I'm so worried about the dogs. How are they?

BOBRITA. Fine. Both mamas whelped a couple of nights ago.

VIOLET. What? You didn't call me??

BOBRITA. *(explaining, to* **GLENDINE***)* Bathsheba and Jezebel. Both litters by the same daddy. So they're half-brothers and sisters. And double cousins.

VIOLET. *(terribly concerned)* Are they all right?

BOBRITA. If we can pull the runt through, we'll get good money off all of them.

VIOLET. Oh! A runt!!

BOBRITA. Twelve pups in each litter.

VIOLET. Twelve! Then I'm naming them for the twelve disciples and the twelve Houses of Israel! We'll cover the Old AND the New Testaments.

*(***LAURA LEE*** comes out. She is tall and handsome. She carries herself with dignity and an easy sense of authority.)*

LAURA LEE. Ladies! Ladies! What in the world is going on here? What are you girls up to?

GLENDINE. We thought we'd help you get a jump on this garden.

LAURA LEE. That's very kind of you, but I'm perfectly capable of handling things on my own.

BOBRITA. We didn't have anything to do waiting for you.

LAURA LEE. Well, I stopped by the old folks home and read them some *Saturday Evening Post.* Then I ran down to the courthouse – I'm working on a genealogy report for Flora Massengale, so I had to wade through all the old birth and death certificates. Then I mailed a letter to Oveta Hobby congratulating her on going from Houston to Washington to take charge of the Women's Army Auxiliary. They'll be doing a lot more than peeling potatoes and folding parachutes – that Oveta Hobby'll have those WAACs whipped into shape!

BOBRITA. The point is you're late.

LAURA LEE. Yes, but you're not going to believe what really delayed me.

VIOLET. What??

LAURA LEE. *(mysteriously)* It happened down at the bus station.

GLENDINE. Did Laverne lock herself in the ticket cage overnight again?

LAURA LEE. No. It's something I found!

VIOLET. You found?

GLENDINE. What is it?

LAURA LEE. Hold on. Close your eyes. I'll go get it.

(*LAURA LEE goes inside.*)

BOBRITA. (*her eyes still open*) What is it?

LAURA LEE. (*from inside*) Are your eyes closed?!

(**BOBRITA** *gives in and closes her eyes.*)

(**LAURA LEE** *comes out with* **IMA JEAN**, *straightening* **IMA JEAN***'s clothes as they walk onto the porch.*)

(**IMA JEAN** *is a little waif of a thing. Eighteen years old, pale and freckled.*)

LAURA LEE (*cont.*) (*to the women*) Now! Open your eyes.

(*complete silence*)

BOBRITA. I repeat – what is it?

LAURA LEE. This is Miss Ima Jean Tatum.

(**IMA JEAN** *acknowledges them with an awkward curtsy.*)

I found Ima Jean waiting at the bus station. She was so sweet, jumped right up to help me.

BOBRITA. Did she have a destination tag or do you get to keep her?

LAURA LEE. Bobrita!

GLENDINE. Precious, what were you doing there?

IMA JEAN. I've been waiting all morning for the four o'clock bus.

BOBRITA. No wonder you look so played out. All the heat for Hell's warmed up in that bus station.

LAURA LEE. Which is why I brought her to the house to wait. Ima Jean, this is Mrs. Tolliver. Her sister, Miss Montgomery. And Mrs. Slocumb.

VIOLET. She's looking a little peaked, Laura Lee.

LAURA LEE. Sweetheart, I'm going to run in and get you a little snack and some lemonade. Do you like it with more lemon or sugar?

IMA JEAN. Sugar, please, ma'am.

(*LAURA LEE goes inside.*)

GLENDINE. Where you coming from, precious?

IMA JEAN. I picked up the bus in Gillette.

BOBRITA. That's way up on the Oklahoma line.

IMA JEAN. Yes, ma'am, I've been riding all night.

VIOLET. Did you get any sleep?

IMA JEAN. Not a lick. The bus kept stopping and stopping. I don't know who all those people were, getting on the bus in the middle of the night. It was spooky. Scared me.

GLENDINE. You need to sit down, precious. You're looking white as the sheeted dead.

IMA JEAN. Oh – I'm fine – really, I am –

(*IMA JEAN faints. The women run to her.*)

BOBRITA. (*calling inside*) Laura Lee! Your surprise has fainted on us!

LAURA LEE. (*from inside*) What??

(*LAURA LEE rushes out with a glass of lemonade and a plate of cold fried chicken.*)

Oh, no! Bobrita, grab that bucket. Glendine, snatch up some washrags from the linen closet –

(*LAURA LEE sits in a chair next to IMA JEAN. She puts IMA JEAN's head on her lap.*)

Violet, get the smelling salts out of the powder room cabinet –

VIOLET. (*running off*) Powder room cabinet – powder room cabinet –

(*BOBRITA is back with the bucket.*)

LAURA LEE. Here, plunge her feet down in it. Ima Jean! Ima Jean, sweetheart!

(**GLENDINE** *runs back with the washrags. She wets one in the bucket, and* **LAURA LEE** *puts it on* **IMA JEAN***'s head.*)

BOBRITA. Throw cold water on her.

GLENDINE. She's not a dog, Bobrita.

LAURA LEE. Breathe for us, darling. Breathe for us.

(**IMA JEAN** *revives.*)

IMA JEAN. Ooh – I feel kind of woozy –

BOBRITA. You're too young to be off by yourself.

GLENDINE. Do your folks know where you are, precious?

LAURA LEE. Have you run off?

IMA JEAN. I don't have any folks. I'm orphaned.

LAURA LEE. (*giving her the chicken*) Which do you like better? White or dark? I gave you the pulley bone and a couple of legs.

IMA JEAN. Either one's fine.

(**IMA JEAN** *falls on the food.*)

LAURA LEE. Now, sweetheart, if you don't have any mama or daddy, who do you live with?

IMA JEAN. I live at the Masonic Home.

LAURA LEE. Over in Gillette?

IMA JEAN. Yes, ma'am.

(**VIOLET** *runs back on from inside.*)

VIOLET. Here they are! Here they are! I've got the smelling salts!

(*She puts the smelling salts under* **IMA JEAN***'s nose, gagging her.* **GLENDINE** *and* **BOBRITA** *pull* **VIOLET** *away.*)

GLENDINE. Violet! Violet!

BOBRITA. She's revived!

VIOLET. Oh.

(**VIOLET** *takes a hit off the smelling salts herself.*)

LAURA LEE. When did you eat last, sweetheart?

IMA JEAN. I fried me up a baloney sandwich last night for the trip, but I made myself only eat half of it. And I had a Mason jar of lemonade to wash it down. But the bus driver swerved – I think he was purposely trying to hit a big ol' armadillo in the road – and that lemonade sloshed all over me and the sack I had my sandwich in. When I fished it out, it wasn't too drownded, so I wrapped it up in my handkerchief and set it on the seat beside me. I nodded off and I reckon it was about three-thirty or four when I woke up and I was kindly famished. So I turned to get my sandwich – and now, you won't believe this part – there was a big ol' fat man sitting where my sandwich used to be. Just a teensy bit of my handkerchief peeking out from under them great big rolls of fat. And I thought, "Oh Lordy, what am I going to do?" He was gone to the world. But you know, hunger does funny things to a person. I had to accept the fact that if I wanted that sandwich, I was going to have to fight for it. Never in my wildest dreams did I imagine I would ever touch that man's fat, but I eased my hand up under there – first one roll – then another – then another – and I lifted. Now you won't believe this part – my sandwich had fallen into the space between the two seats! It was wedged in there tighter than a tick. It was safe! So with one hand, I kept that fat lifted up and with the other, I ever so gently eased my sandwich out. And just as I got it, the bus pulls into a station and the fat man wakes up with a big snort. Starts flailing his arms around. Knocked the sandwich right out of my hand. But then the driver opens the door and the floor lights come on. And I seen it. There it was, away up front. And now, you won't believe this part – my handkerchief was nowhere to be seen. My sandwich was laying there nekkid on the bus floor. And just as I'm creeping up there for it, here comes a blind man with a big ol' dog, scarfed it right down. So yes, ma'am, I'm a mite hungry.

(Stunned silence greets the tale. Finally –)

BOBRITA. Well, I don't begrudge the dog.

LAURA LEE. Ima Jean, sweetheart, you must be exhausted.

IMA JEAN. Yes, ma'am, I'm pretty much wore out.

LAURA LEE. We're about to have a meeting, sweetheart. Why don't you run upstairs, lie down, get out of this heat. First bedroom at the top of the stairs. The chenille bedspread with the peacock pattern.

IMA JEAN. Oh. Thank you, ma'am. I'll be as silent as the Sphinx.

*(**IMA JEAN** takes her plate and goes inside.)*

LAURA LEE. *(leading the way into the yard)* Ladies, shall we? –

(The women assemble at a wicker table.)

GLENDINE. Isn't she a funny little thing?

BOBRITA. Pitiful.

VIOLET. A little waif loose in the world.

LAURA LEE. She broke my heart when I saw her all by herself at the bus station. I couldn't just leave her there. I call this meeting of the Eufala Springs Garden Club to order.

*(**GLENDINE** runs to get a bag she brought in with her. She scoots back to her chair with the bag in her lap.)*

The first order of business is the reading of the minutes.

*(**VIOLET** stands. Meanwhile, **GLENDINE** starts taking sewing supplies out of her bag. She takes out a big piece of blue satin and shakes it out during the reading of the minutes.)*

VIOLET. "March 2, 1942. At the home of Mrs. Bobrita Montgomery. Meeting of the Eufala –"

BOBRITA. We were all there.

VIOLET. Out of order.

LAURA LEE. Bobrita.

VIOLET. "March 2, 1942. At the home of –"

BOBRITA. I move we approve the minutes.

GLENDINE. *(quickly)* Second the motion.

LAURA LEE. So moved.

VIOLET. *(wilting in her chair)* But –

LAURA LEE. The next order of business before the assembly is the fund-raising Gala.

(**GLENDINE** *snips the piece of satin, then rips it loudly.*)

Glendine, could you hold off on that?

GLENDINE. Oh, don't mind me.

LAURA LEE. Suggestions from members-at-large accepted.

BOBRITA. The first order of business is getting this yard in order.

VIOLET. *(pulling out a copy of Robert's Rules of Order)* You have to make a motion to introduce an item to the chair –

LAURA LEE. This yard? I know things are a bit disheveled, but I'm called upon to notarize so many things and I'm helping with the first grade diphtheria shots –

BOBRITA. You've taken that on, too?

GLENDINE. *(to* **BOBRITA***)* Couldn't those big strapping twins of yours help us?

BOBRITA. No, Travis and Crockett are off rodeoing up in Claremore, Oklahoma. Laura Lee, this garden is nowhere near ready. Look at that latticework, look at the porch, look at –

LAURA LEE. Bobrita, I don't need any free advice from you.

BOBRITA. The Gala's only a month away.

GLENDINE. We're all willing to help. Of course, I'm under the gun to get these pep squad costumes finished. I haven't even commenced sewing on all the bluebonnets.

LAURA LEE. When I get time, I know just how I want everything.

BOBRITA. There are other places we can have it, Laura Lee. Like out at my ranch.

LAURA LEE. We're not breaking with tradition. I've always managed before.

GLENDINE. But you had R.L. to help you.

LAURA LEE. *(bristling)* Ladies! I'm not dependent on you or anyone. Meeting adjourned.

VIOLET. But – but – out of order – out of order –

*(The telephone rings. **LAURA LEE** strides up to the porch as the others continue to protest.)*

BOBRITA. Laura Lee!

GLENDINE. We're not finished!

BOBRITA. Some decisions need to be made here!

*(**LAURA LEE** reaches inside the window and pulls out a candlestick telephone.)*

LAURA LEE. Hello…Oh yes, Mildred Ann, I've got your chart right here.

(to the women)

Excuse me, ladies. This is one of my clients.

(on the telephone)

The happy news is the impending lunar eclipse means increasing luck in your love life. Mercury in retrograde will make the blood rise. Romance will ensue!… No, honey, he's just tired. Send the children to your mother's and fix him a chicken-fried steak. That'll build him up.… Let me hear from you.

*(**LAURA LEE** addresses the women from the porch.)*

Now if you'll excuse me, I've got a big bowl of potato salad to make for poor ol' Polly. She stumbled over one of her cats.

BOBRITA. Laura Lee! You've got all you can say grace over now. We've got to get back to the business at hand – this Gala. And this yard –

LAURA LEE. *(firmly)* I'm getting to it.

GLENDINE. We're under a deadline, Laura Lee.

LAURA LEE. I believe I've been giving the Garden Club Gala in this yard for the last thirty-five years.

*(**IMA JEAN** has stepped out onto the porch.)*

IMA JEAN. Excuse me –

LAURA LEE. Oh! Did you get a little rest, sweetheart?

IMA JEAN. I expect I'd better be heading to the bus station.

LAURA LEE. Sweetheart, there's not another bus until four o'clock. That's a long wait.

GLENDINE. Where are you headed?

IMA JEAN. Oh, I'm not going anywhere. I'm waiting on somebody. And I'm afraid I'll miss him if –

GLENDINE. Him?

VIOLET. You're meeting a man?

GLENDINE. Ooh, tell us who.

IMA JEAN. My beloved. Jesse.

GLENDINE. Your beloved! Adorable!

(to the others)

She calls him her beloved!

VIOLET. Right out of the Song of Solomon: "My beloved is mine and I am his!"

GLENDINE. (to **IMA JEAN**) How come you're meeting him here in Eufala Springs, precious?

IMA JEAN. We're heading to Galveston. He lives on the other side of the state and this was the easiest place to meet up.

VIOLET. What's in Galveston?

IMA JEAN. Jesse's an infantryman. He's shipping off tomorrow morning, so we're getting married here at the courthouse this afternoon.

GLENDINE. Married?!

LAURA LEE. Oh, sweetheart!

GLENDINE. Were you going to change your clothes at the bus station?

IMA JEAN. No, ma'am.

VIOLET. You were going to wait and change at the courthouse?

IMA JEAN. No, ma'am.

BOBRITA. Well, where?

IMA JEAN. I was just fixing to wear what I've got on.

GLENDINE. Oh.

VIOLET. I haven't been to a wedding since last spring when Floy Kate Williams married that Yankee she met on that archeological bone-hunt out in Big Bend.

GLENDINE. Precious, can I be your witness?

BOBRITA. Now that may not be the most auspicious beginning.

(*to* **IMA JEAN**, *about* **GLENDINE**)

She's on number six or seven.

GLENDINE. It just means I have the most experience. And please remember that I was widowed once.

BOBRITA. Which one was that? The rodeo announcer or the Smooth-as-Silk stocking salesman?

GLENDINE. Don't start on him. He kept you all in silk stockings the whole year I was married to him.

VIOLET. Can I be your witness AND sing? You're going to need me to sing.

LAURA LEE. Ladies, ladies! The first order of business is to get a minister over to the courthouse.

VIOLET. Bobrita can call St. Andrews and get Reverend Witherspoon.

BOBRITA. I doubt an Episcopal priest would marry somebody outside the church.

GLENDINE. I'll call Preacher Jackson down at Brush Arbor.

VIOLET. Didn't Brush Arbor just break off?

BOBRITA. You know Baptists – get mad at each other, walk across the street, start a new church.

LAURA LEE. I'll call Pastor Abbott over at Wesleyan.

VIOLET. Maybe that's not a good idea.

LAURA LEE. What's wrong with the Methodists?

VIOLET. Oh, not a thing. But his wife was married before.

(*quickly, to* **GLENDINE**)

Not that that makes her a bad person.

LAURA LEE. *(to* **IMA JEAN***)* What denomination are you, sweetheart?

IMA JEAN. Oh, I'm not afflicted with any denomination. But Jesse's a Seventh-Day Advantage.

LAURA LEE. We'll just get Judge Hamilton to marry them.

VIOLET. I don't believe we can all fit in that little registry office.

LAURA LEE. You can get married in the courtroom. I was the Mayor's wife for thirty-five years – I can certainly get us the courtroom.

BOBRITA. My Martha Washingtons are putting on a show. I could bring those to spruce the place up.

GLENDINE. And my stephanotis is in bloom. Should we have candles? Will it be dark enough? I can bring my crystal candlesticks.

BOBRITA. No, I'll bring my sterling candelabra –

LAURA LEE. I'll start a list –

(writing)

– Martha Washingtons – stephanotis –

VIOLET. How are we going to get everything down to the courthouse?

GLENDINE. There's no reason we can't have candlesticks AND your candelabra.

BOBRITA. We don't need both. It's a civil ceremony.

LAURA LEE. *(writing)* – candelabra – candlesticks –

GLENDINE. What about the cake?

LAURA LEE. I'll make a coconut cake.

VIOLET. It'll have to be a sheet cake. They cook quicker.

GLENDINE. But shouldn't it be round – for eternal love?

BOBRITA. Hot as it is, moving it over there, all that icing –

GLENDINE. What about punch?

LAURA LEE. *(writing)* Oh, dear – punch –

GLENDINE. How are we going to keep it cold?

BOBRITA. This is getting to be awfully involved.

VIOLET. Who's going to bring the punch bowl?

LAURA LEE. – a punch bowl –

BOBRITA. Sister, that can be your responsibility.

VIOLET. I can't carry Grandma Bertha's crystal punch bowl and eleven cups up the courthouse steps. That'll throw my back right out.

BOBRITA. Would you rather bring the forks? That should be manageable.

LAURA LEE. *(writing like mad)* – silverware –

BOBRITA. We've got to have dessert plates. And napkins.

LAURA LEE. – plates – linens –

GLENDINE. Mine aren't ironed.

BOBRITA. We're going to use up all our gas coupons getting things over there.

LAURA LEE. Ladies! Ladies! Wait just a minute! – Just a minute! — I've got it!

GLENDINE. Got what?

LAURA LEE. The perfect solution!

BOBRITA. What now?

LAURA LEE. This is a stroke of genius, ladies. I can't believe I didn't think of it earlier.

(A beat. They all look at her expectantly.)

We'll have the wedding right here!

*(**GLENDINE** squeals, **BOBRITA** groans, and **VIOLET** slips into a chair, fanning herself.)*

(CURTAIN)

Scene 2

*(At rise, **IMA JEAN** is sitting in a chair in the garden.
GLENDINE is putting her hair in rag rolls. **LAURA LEE**
is on the telephone on the porch. The women all wear
aprons.)*

*(From inside, **VIOLET** sings "O Promise Me.")*

LAURA LEE. I'm telling you, Evelyn, your ecliptic is looking
mighty ragged. You tell Horace to stay home with you
and call off that trip to Port Aransas to go deep-sea
fishing –

(From inside, a dissonant chord on the piano.)

(calling into the house) Put the cover down on the keys!
Be careful turning that tight corner!

(on the telephone)

– Tell Horace to go next month when Pisces is rising.
That's the fish sign –

(calling inside)

– Don't try and squeeze it through the breakfast room
door! –

(on the telephone)

– And one more thing – if you're going on a diet, don't
start it until the solar eclipse –

BOBRITA. *(calling out)* Has this piano been tuned?

LAURA LEE. Yes, Bobrita, and the toilets work.

(on the telephone)

– But then again, if you've got that much weight to
lose, you might need to get the jump on it.

*(**LAURA LEE** hangs up as **BOBRITA** and **VIOLET** appear,
rolling the piano onto the porch. **BOBRITA** pushes from
behind while **VIOLET** steers from the front.)*

Swing that end around! Careful! Don't hit the railing!
Let me do it.

(**VIOLET** *keeps singing "O Promise Me."*)

BOBRITA. Sister! Tone that down until we get this thing in place.

LAURA LEE. *(working on her list)* We're going to need a big bouquet on top of the piano. And another on the refreshment table. And another on this table.

(**VIOLET** *sinks onto one of the stacks of papers on the porch, winded from the piano-moving.*)

BOBRITA. I can put my glads on the serving table.

GLENDINE. I've got loads of bridal's wreath. And baskets of bleeding hearts.

LAURA LEE. We can make Ima Jean's nosegay out of my lily-of-the-valley and surround it with Queen Anne's lace –

BOBRITA. Queen Anne's lace wilts.

LAURA LEE. We'll use my baby's breath. And my rambling roses.

BOBRITA. Your roses have rambled too far.

(**BOBRITA** *picks up the telephone and dials.*)

VIOLET. Ima Jean, honey, what kind of flowers do you like?

IMA JEAN. At the Home, we had zinnias and nasturtiums and geraniums –

BOBRITA. Surely we can do better than that.

(on the telephone)

Ascensia, tell Pepe to cut me a big bucket of Martha Washingtons and glads and –

VIOLET. Are you sure you want Martha Washingtons? They're just a crown of thorns. There are some red ramblers on the south side –

BOBRITA. Tell him to bring some red ramblers –

VIOLET. The magnolia leaves –

BOBRITA. Some magnolia leaves –

VIOLET. Snapdragons –

BOBRITA. Snapdragons. Just whatever's blooming.

VIOLET. Then go over to Glendine's –

BOBRITA. Then over by Mrs. Slocumb's back door, bring us her stephanotis, lily-of-the-valley – oh, just bring everything she's got. Jump right on it. Oh, and Ascencia! Did you find those registry papers for the dogs? I'm going to need them to sell the pups.

VIOLET. Tell her to look in my hope chest. Which you hauled out to that little cabin in the wilderness you banished me to.

BOBRITA. *(on the telephone)* Look in the little house in Miss Violet's hope chest.

LAURA LEE. Tell her to send over your sugar. I've just about used up my ration.

BOBRITA. Bring my sugar from the pantry – all of it. And look under Miss Violet's bed and bring that little sack of sugar she keeps squirreled away.

(She hangs up.)

VIOLET. But, Sister –

BOBRITA. Don't Sister me, Sister. Laura Lee, we can't leave these papers and junk here this afternoon.

LAURA LEE. *(on a step-stool, pruning)* Don't touch any of it. I'm in the middle of sorting it.

VIOLET. The war effort needs it now, Laura Lee.

LAURA LEE. I'm getting to it. Throw a quilt over it if you can't stand it. There's some quilts upstairs in Mother's trunk.

BOBRITA. Sister! Rouse yourself and come help me.

VIOLET. Now, Sister, I can't carry anything too heavy.

*(With **BOBRITA** and **VIOLET** gone, **GLENDINE** ambushes **LAURA LEE**.)*

GLENDINE. Laura Lee, what can I say to Violet to get her to leave? If we spend one more evening doing jigsaw puzzles and hearing about her plantar's wart, Coach is going to throw a wall-eyed fit.

*(to **IMA JEAN**)*

Am I pulling too hard, precious?

IMA JEAN. No, ma'am, I'm real hard-headed.

GLENDINE. Life with Coach was a pink cloud until she moved in. Now we never get a minute to ourselves. Poor Bobrita.

LAURA LEE. Poor Bobrita!?

GLENDINE. Now I know why she's so short-tempered.

(*to* **IMA JEAN**)

Precious, whatever you do, don't live with Jesse's people. I've been down that road when I married Mario. My second husband. Laid claim to being a count. Of course, every Italian barber claims to be a count. Whisked me off to Sicily to live with his mother and four unmarried sisters. He was the only one in the family without a moustache. I got over there and found out he was no 'count – literally.

(**BOBRITA** *and* **VIOLET** *return, loaded down with quilts.* **VIOLET** *sinks onto a stack of newspapers and fans herself as* **GLENDINE** *continues her tale.*)

The only good thing I got out of that marriage was my wedding dress. Lace made by the nuns. Real seed pearls and a long illusion veil.

BOBRITA. Sister, toss that one with the wedding ring pattern over the newspapers. At least it'll fit the occasion. Now, Laura Lee, throwing quilts around may serve us for today, but not for the Gala.

IMA JEAN. What's a Gala?

GLENDINE. Oh, it's a big soiree!

(**IMA JEAN** *is even more puzzled.*)

LAURA LEE. It's a big elegant party. We use it to raise money for noble causes.

BOBRITA. I think we might have sent a contribution up to Gillette one year.

VIOLET. We've been having it here at Laura Lee's house for thirty-five years. Every year she and her husband R.L. would –

(She trails off. An awkward pause.)

LAURA LEE. Glendine, get on the other end of this serving table and help me move it down into the yard.

IMA JEAN. I can do it.

LAURA LEE. No, no, sweetheart, we wouldn't dream of letting you do it. You're the bride.

IMA JEAN. I'm used to hard work at the Masonic Home.

VIOLET. How long were you there, honey?

IMA JEAN. Since I was six.

GLENDINE. Oh, precious. How'd you come to be there?

IMA JEAN. On account of the Dust Bowl. My folks dropped me there 'cause they needed to travel light. They was going to send for me when they got settled. After a couple of years, I quit waiting for them.

VIOLET. *(her arms around* **IMA JEAN***)* Oh, honey, you're so alone –

BOBRITA. Hold on, Laura Lee, I'll move the ladder for you.

LAURA LEE. I've got it.

IMA JEAN. *(to* **VIOLET***)* No, ma'am. I'm not alone no more. I got Jesse.

GLENDINE. *(teasing her)* Ooh, Jesse. I'd be wary of a boy named Jesse.

IMA JEAN. No, ma'am. He's true blue.

LAURA LEE. Where'd you meet him, sweetheart?

IMA JEAN. At the state fair last September. He was at the FFA barn. He'd brung his goats. He had five – Annette, Cecile, Emelie, Marie, and Yvonne – named after the Dionne Quints. He'd harness them to a cart, they'd pull little kids around. I was in charge of the littler ones from the Home. And do you know Jesse got every one of them kids a cotton candy? Just so generous and kind. And let them play with the baby goats. Him and me visited all evening long. Then a few days later – now you're not going to believe this part – he stopped by to see me at the Home. He was hauling his goats back, so he couldn't stay too long – you know goats stink.

BOBRITA. I can certainly understand how you'd fall for a boy like that.

IMA JEAN. But he was already promised to a girl back in his hometown. Jimmie Sue. Her folks and his are real good friends. Her daddy's rich – cattle and oil. I hear tell she's real pretty when she's not broke out with the infantigo.

VIOLET. When did you see him next?

IMA JEAN. Christmastime. The Masonic Home puts on a great big pageant, and lo and behold if he didn't bring his goats and lambs clear across the state for the shepherds in the field keeping watch over their flock by night. He put his hand over mine on the hymnal, pretending like he was helping me hold it. I just kept singing, "Field and fountain, moor and mountain, following yonder star."

GLENDINE. Then what?

IMA JEAN. Then last month, he escorted me to my Senior Dance. He'd just graduated and was about to enlist. We were dancing to "I'll Hold You in My Heart 'til I Can Hold You in My Arms" when he leaned over and whispered that he'd broke up with Jimmie Sue. That's when he asked me to marry him. And that's why I'm not alone no more.

LAURA LEE. Well, what a romance. I've never heard anything quite like it.

BOBRITA. Who has?

GLENDINE. Laura Lee, tell about how R.L. proposed to you!

(A silence.)

(Then a knock at the gate.)

LAURA LEE. *(rushing to the gate)* I bet that's Pepe with the flowers.

(The women go to the gate, leaving **IMA JEAN** *alone.)*

(at the gate) Pour some of that water off. It's sloshing everywhere.

GLENDINE. I want to keep these roses immersed up to their necks.

VIOLET. Pepe, are the babies all right? Don't let the other pups push out the runt. I'm worried sick about him.

(They return with buckets of flowers and sacks of sugar.)

(to **BOBRITA***)* If they push him out, promise me you'll feed him every two hours with a doll bottle.

BOBRITA. A doll bottle! Then he'd think I was his mama.

VIOLET. Oh, I love it when they think I'm their mama.

(to **IMA JEAN***)*

Like our old bloodhound Samson. I brushed his teeth, painted his nails – dew claws included – and put Old Spice behind his ears every morning. I gave that dog everything but eternal life.

LAURA LEE. *(to* **GLENDINE***)* Set those here.

(They set the buckets of flowers on the steps and start inside.)

IMA JEAN. *(to* **BOBRITA***)* What kind of dogs?

BOBRITA. Blue tick, redbones, blue heelers, coon dogs – all kind of hounds.

LAURA LEE. *(gesturing the women into the house)* Ladies, we've got to get on the refreshments.

IMA JEAN. What can I do?

LAURA LEE. Oh. Well – you can put these flowers in vases.

*(***IMA JEAN** *is once again left alone. Inside the kitchen window, the women start making preparations.)*

Violet, reach up there and get me my mixing bowls down. Glendine, start separating those eggs.

BOBRITA. Save the yolks for me. I'll give them to the mama-dogs.

LAURA LEE. Oh, no, you don't. I'm not giving up my yolks to a bunch of dogs. I'll use them in the custard for the ice cream. Violet, pull open that drawer and get us some measuring spoons. Bobrita, put me on a pot to boil so we can skin the peaches.

GLENDINE. What do you think of lemon cake? Or spice cake?

VIOLET. That's just blasphemous for a wedding cake. Why don't we serve Scripture Cake? Sift three cups of Exodus 29:2, then cream a stick of Judges 5:25 with three cups of –

BOBRITA. Sister, that's Hell to cook.

VIOLET. How would you know? I don't know how poor Beaumont's gotten along the last three weeks. Cooking's never been your stronghold.

BOBRITA. Sister, go outside and practice your singing.

VIOLET. Well. I'll just do that.

(*VIOLET comes out and sees* **IMA JEAN** *working on the bouquets. She gasps.*)

Oh, no! Girls, some assistance is needed out here –

(*The other women run out.*)

BOBRITA. What is it now?

LAURA LEE. (*gently, to* **IMA JEAN**) Oh, dear. Sweetheart, these have to be mixed. We're going to have mixed bouquets.

IMA JEAN. I'm sorry.

LAURA LEE. That's all right, sweetheart. Glendine, see if you can't help her.

(**GLENDINE** *sets to arranging the flowers as* **LAURA LEE** *and* **BOBRITA** *head back to the kitchen.* **VIOLET** *starts practicing "O Promise Me."*)

BOBRITA. (*at the door*) Violet, you're sharp!

VIOLET. I am not.

BOBRITA. (*to* **LAURA LEE** *as they head inside*) She's always sharp. Flat's bad enough, but sharp will clear a room.

GLENDINE. (*to* **IMA JEAN**) Oh, precious, how I envy you. You're entering the most romantic time of your life. The first few months are when I enjoy my marriages most. When I married the cruise ship captain, it was nothing but tender moments – standing by the railing looking at the moon on the water. Until I found out he was having those same tender moments with his wife in Caracas and his wife in Havana.

BOBRITA. *(calling from inside)* You forgot his wife in Vera-cruz.

GLENDINE. That one he wasn't married to.

*(to **IMA JEAN**)*

My point is there's nothing more dreamy than the moon on the water. So you and Jesse should stay in my lakehouse tonight! It's an ideal place for a honeymoon. So deliciously private –

BOBRITA. That shack is covered in dirt-dauber nests!

(coming out)

The place for them to stay is my new little house, the one we built for Sister. It's the perfect honeymoon hideaway. You and Jesse can come there straight after the reception.

(She picks up the telephone and dials.)

GLENDINE. But – but my lakehouse is charming –

BOBRITA. If you like sharing it with a family of raccoons.

GLENDINE. It's been good enough for four generations.

BOBRITA. That's my point.

(on the telephone)

Ascensia, put a bouquet of honeysuckle in the bed-room of Miss Violet's little house...No, she's not coming home...And dig out my wedding sheets...I don't know where they are.

VIOLET. The bottom drawer of Mama's secretary.

BOBRITA. They're in the secretary.

(She hangs up and heads back inside.)

GLENDINE. *(crushed)* I thought my lakehouse was sweet.

*(**VIOLET**, indignant on **GLENDINE**'s behalf, follows **BOBRITA** inside. **GLENDINE**, near tears, trails along, leaving **IMA JEAN** alone once again.)*

VIOLET. *(hot on* **BOBRITA***'s heels)* Well, as usual, Sister, you get your own way. At the expense of the feelings of others.

BOBRITA. I get my own way because I've got a better solution.

GLENDINE. *(wounded)* Must be wonderful to know you're always right.

LAURA LEE. *(over the bickering women)* Ladies, let's all save our energy for the task at hand! Putting on this wedding in one afternoon is not going to be easy!

(Hearing this, **IMA JEAN** *starts taking the rag rolls out of her hair.)*

(in the kitchen) Now, we've got to start that cake. Where's the sugar?

BOBRITA. Hand it over, Sister.

(IMA JEAN *quietly gathers her valise, then heads down the porch steps. She exits through the gate.)*

GLENDINE. Do we have to have boiled icing? I think we can have confectioners sugar icing.

LAURA LEE. This is the most important day in the child's life. I think we can make boiled icing. Ima Jean, you want some lemonade? – Violet, start greasing those cake pans – Ima Jean, sweetheart? –

*(***LAURA LEE** *comes out onto the porch.)*

Ima Jean?

(She surveys the empty yard.)

Ima Jean?

(CURTAIN)

Scene 3

(At rise, no one is onstage.)

*(***LAURA LEE*** *runs on. Obviously distressed, she takes a moment to fan herself with her hat before starting off again. The telephone rings. She rushes back to catch it.)*

LAURA LEE *(cont.)* Hello...Lucille, you won't believe the furor going on around here. I haven't stopped...No, I can't get to your love life until this weekend. In the meantime, my advice to you – and this is not as your astrologer, but as your friend – is just set the mood with some Bing Crosby, put on some White Shoulders, and hope for the best.

(She hangs up. **GLENDINE** *and* **VIOLET** *rush in –* **VIOLET** *is holding a hatbox and* **GLENDINE** *is carrying a stack of them.)*

Did you find her? Was she anywhere on the square?

VIOLET. We didn't see a sign of her.

GLENDINE. Not in Juandell's Beauty Boutique, not in Evelyn's Shoes –

LAURA LEE. Did you look in Wanda's Whatnots?

GLENDINE. Everywhere. We didn't find Ima Jean, but I ran across the most gorgeous hats on sale.

VIOLET. I bought one, too. I know vanity's a sin but –

GLENDINE. Just wear it to church. That'll cancel it out.

LAURA LEE. You two are just like Mrs. Miniver buying that hat she didn't need.

VIOLET. Oh, don't talk about Mrs. Miniver – you'll make me cry.

GLENDINE. Did you see where Mr. Churchill said Greer Garson's done more for the war effort than six divisions of fighting men?

VIOLET. Oh, Laura Lee, you won't believe. Every shop we went into, they had piles of stuff stacked up they could be sending to the war effort.

LAURA LEE. See? I don't feel so bad now.

GLENDINE. Oh, and we ran into Irene Corbin. I hate to tell you, but you've stirred up a hornet's nest with that genealogy you've taken up. She says you've got her related to Myrtle Corbin.

VIOLET. The Texas four-legged woman!

LAURA LEE. Well, what difference does it make? It's on her husband's side.

VIOLET. *(terribly worried)* But what if it's inherited?

(From inside, we hear **BOBRITA.** *)*

BOBRITA. I got her!

VIOLET. The lost are found!

*(***BOBRITA*** *brings* **IMA JEAN** *out.)*

LAURA LEE. Ima Jean! Where'd you find her?

BOBRITA. In the Baptist Church. It dawned on me – look for a place with oscillating fans.

LAURA LEE. Sweetheart, why'd you run off?

IMA JEAN. I'm just causing you so much trouble. You're doing all this for me and I don't have any way to repay you.

LAURA LEE. Sweetheart, we don't expect you to.

IMA JEAN. But the cake and the ice cream and the flowers –

LAURA LEE. It's our pleasure, sweetheart.

GLENDINE. All the people on the square are excited about it.

VIOLET. The shopgirls. Judge Hamilton. Even the new Mayor and his wife. We told them to come at seven when it's cooler.

BOBRITA. It's going to be a regular hair-pull.

LAURA LEE. Next on our list is to find you a wedding dress.

BOBRITA. She can wear mine. It'll fit her perfect. I was thinner then.

(raised eyebrows)

GLENDINE. I have one!

BOBRITA. You have several.

GLENDINE. The prettiest is the one I wore the second time I married the self-collapsible umbrella inventor.

VIOLET. But that dress was shell pink, not white.

BOBRITA. Appropriately.

GLENDINE. What about the one when I married the undertaker?

BOBRITA. Smells like formaldehyde.

VIOLET. You could wear my debutante dress.

BOBRITA. Sister, it'd take two days to starch and iron all that organdy.

GLENDINE. Laura Lee, what about your dress?

(A beat, then –)

LAURA LEE. – I don't want that custard to go bad in this heat. All those egg yolks.

(LAURA LEE goes inside.)

GLENDINE. Oh dear, I hope I didn't say the wrong thing.

BOBRITA. She's just still so shut-down about it. – I better hurry home and dig out my dress.

GLENDINE. And I can bring back a selection. What size shoe do you wear, precious?

IMA JEAN. Seven.

GLENDINE. Perfect.

BOBRITA. *(to GLENDINE as they go out the gate)* Leave that Sicilian gypsy rig at home.

GLENDINE. You better watch out or I'll bring back my tambourine.

(As they leave, LAURA LEE brings out the ice cream churn.)

IMA JEAN. Miss Laura Lee, let me help you.

LAURA LEE. Thank you, sweetheart, but I'm fine. I'll go get the ice.

(to VIOLET as she goes inside, indicating a big bag under the porch)

Violet, get that bag of rock salt from under the porch there.

IMA JEAN. Here, let me get it.

VIOLET. *(sinking into a chair)* Thank you, dear.

> *(IMA JEAN pulls out the bag as LAURA LEE returns with a big bowl of ice.)*

LAURA LEE. Violet!

VIOLET. It's just so hard for me to stoop.

LAURA LEE. *(to IMA JEAN)* Thank you, sweetheart.

> *(as LAURA LEE starts to layer ice around the canister in the churn with the rock salt –)*

I've forgotten how much to use. R.L. always – he would –

(She trails off. Then –)

IMA JEAN. It's all right, Miss Laura Lee. I know how to do it.

> *(LAURA LEE turns away. She hurries back inside.)*

> *(IMA JEAN starts layering ice and rock salt as VIOLET sits and fans herself.)*

VIOLET. Poor thing. 'Course you don't know what she was like before R.L. – before he –

(pressing on)

She was always busy, always helping people, but now she's – I don't know – different. She distracts herself with all these projects – but they're all mixed up and none of them ever get done.

IMA JEAN. What was Mr. R.L. like?

VIOLET. Ooh, the handsomest man in Eufala Springs. And he adored Laura Lee. Now THAT was a wedding.

(still disappointed)

Of course, Sister was the matron of honor. We all wanted to be maid of honor – me, Glendine, Sister – but you can only pick one, you know. And Sister had just married Laura Lee's brother Beaumont, so of course Laura Lee had to pick her.

(**IMA JEAN** *stops layering the ice and salt in the churn as she becomes absorbed in* **VIOLET**'*s telling.*)

VIOLET *(cont.)* Anyway, they were the most fun couple you'd ever want to be around. People still talk about how, after their wedding, the whole congregation fell right in behind them, up the aisle, down the steps, around the square, and down to the lake. We set up such a racket all the dogs in town commenced to howling! When we got down to the lake there was a fireworks display, all the colors reflecting in the water. So beautiful –

(**VIOLET** *abruptly changes the subject as* **LAURA LEE** *hurries out with a stack of dessert plates and sets them on the serving table.* **IMA JEAN** *quickly goes back to setting up the churn.*)

VIOLET *(cont.)* *(loudly covering for* **LAURA LEE**'*s benefit)* Well, you know, Sister and I aren't the only ones. They say Constance and Joan Bennett don't even speak to each other. Same with Olivia de Havilland and Joan Fontaine. Sister and I at least speak to each other.

(**LAURA LEE** *scurries back inside.*)

(conspiratorially, to **IMA JEAN***)* It was last August. It devastated everybody – the whole town.

IMA JEAN. *(stopping her work on the ice cream churn)* What happened?

VIOLET. R.L. disappeared.

IMA JEAN. Disappeared?

VIOLET. Not a trace.

(**LAURA LEE** *runs out with silverware.*)

(loudly covering again as **IMA JEAN** *finishes the ice cream preparation)* You know, Sister hates those teensy dogs. She's refused for years to let me get a lapdog. I want a little Scottie dog like Fala. Or a little white fluffy dog I could dye pink for Easter.

(**LAURA LEE** *heads back inside.*)

VIOLET *(cont.)* *(to* **IMA JEAN***)* You remember that awful hurricane in Matagorda? It was like Hell with the lid kicked off. Well, word went out for volunteers. So of course R.L. and his volunteer firemen were the first to respond. He rounded them all up – Coach, Beaumont, the whole bunch – and headed for the Gulf. Awful. Snakes, dead cattle. Like God's wrath. R.L. commandeered a rowboat and took off into water so high people were on top of their houses. The winds were whipping, rain still pouring down. He sees a pregnant woman holding onto her little boy for dear life. He manages to get them in his boat – despite there being no room for him – and pushes them off. Said to send the boat back for him. But nobody saw him after that.

IMA JEAN. Oh, no.

*(***LAURA LEE*** *has come out the door with the iced wedding cake. She stops and listens, unnoticed by* **VIOLET** *and* **IMA JEAN***.)*

VIOLET. We gathered here every day and waited, not knowing anything, fearing the worst. Laura Lee looked after all of us – protected us – it just comes natural to her. Then when the men drove up, and Beaumont climbed those front steps –

(She stops, overwhelmed with the telling.)

Forgive me, honey. We all just have to keep it bottled up. Laura Lee never even had a service for R.L. – wouldn't let us give him one – even when her daughter Lily came over from Abilene and begged her. She never talked about it. Just went around town, like you see her, involving herself in other people's lives.

IMA JEAN. Now I feel even worse including in on her.

VIOLET. Honey, please don't deny her – or the rest of us – the pleasure of this day.

*(***BOBRITA*** *and* **GLENDINE*** *run in with wedding dresses.* **LAURA LEE** *slips back inside with the cake.)*

BOBRITA. *(to* **IMA JEAN***)* Jump up here, child. Let's try this on you.

IMA JEAN. But –

BOBRITA. Nobody can see you.

GLENDINE. Ain't nobody here but us chickens.

(GLENDINE hangs her dresses in a row on the porch as BOBRITA helps IMA JEAN out of her own dress and into BOBRITA's dress. IMA JEAN wears a modest cotton slip with broad straps.)

(VIOLET sits on the ice cream churn and watches the proceedings.)

(LAURA LEE re-enters with the wedding cake.)

LAURA LEE. The radio says it's raining over in Fairview.

BOBRITA. We could use rain.

LAURA LEE. Yes, but not today!

(LAURA LEE runs over to give the churn a crank every now and then. GLENDINE and BOBRITA also turn it whenever they pass VIOLET sitting on it.)

BOBRITA. Glendine, grab the other end of this tablecloth.

(BOBRITA's dress falls right off of IMA JEAN.)

IMA JEAN. Uh-oh.

VIOLET. Sister, I guess you weren't as thin as you thought you were.

GLENDINE. *(running over to IMA JEAN)* Let's try this on you, precious.

VIOLET. Should I run down and get Jesse?

LAURA LEE. Call Laverne down at the bus station. Tell her to send him this way.

GLENDINE. I'll call her.

(picking up the telephone)

How's she going to know him?

LAURA LEE. Sweetheart, can you tell us what he looks like?

IMA JEAN. *(taking a deep breath to start one of her tales)* Well, now his family on his mama's side –

LAURA LEE. Just a thumbnail sketch, sweetheart.

GLENDINE. *(on the telephone)* Laverne, we want you look for
– hold on –

IMA JEAN. Well, he's real handsome.

BOBRITA. Could you be a little more specific?

IMA JEAN. He's in his infantry uniform.

LAURA LEE. What color's his hair?

IMA JEAN. He's almost a carrot-top.

LAURA LEE. How tall is he?

IMA JEAN. About this much taller than me.

LAURA LEE. *(to GLENDINE)* Say five-ten.

GLENDINE. *(on the telephone)* An infantryman. Five-ten, red-
headed. Send him down to Mrs. McInerney's when he
gets off the bus –

(IMA JEAN has put on one of GLENDINE's dresses.)

BOBRITA. Oh, Lord. That looks like the dress is wearing
you.

GLENDINE. – Oh! She says the bus is pulling in now!

(She hangs up and runs over to help IMA JEAN.)

Try this one!

LAURA LEE. *(kicking into high gear)* Bobrita, bring those vases
down.

BOBRITA. *(vases in hand)* Isn't this too tall?

LAURA LEE. It's buffet-style. Nobody's sitting down. Now,
let's get on this bunting.

BOBRITA. This has been crumpled up since last Fourth of
July.

GLENDINE. Oh, dear. Does it need ironing?

LAURA LEE. The wrinkles will hang out.

VIOLET. I'm not sure bunting's appropriate for a wedding.

BOBRITA. Nonsense. The groom's one of our brave boys in
uniform.

VIOLET. This porch needs to be swept.

BOBRITA. Hosed down.

GLENDINE. Where do you want these bleeding hearts?

LAURA LEE. There are hooks on the porch. Put two on each side.

BOBRITA. It doesn't have to be formally balanced, Laura Lee. We're not inaugurating the Mayor.

LAURA LEE. Bobrita, this is a formal occasion. We're not going to slight this child just because we're short on time.

(The telephone rings.)

Hello…Yes, Laverne…What? Are you sure?…Oh, dear.

*(**LAURA LEE** hangs up. She turns to the other women.)*

He wasn't on the bus.

*(A thunderclap. The women look up at the sky as **IMA JEAN** faints out from under the wedding dress.)*

(SLOW CURTAIN)

ACT TWO

(At rise, **LAURA LEE**, **BOBRITA**, **VIOLET**, *and* **GLEN-DINE** *are on the porch eating ice cream out of china bowls.* **BOBRITA** *takes the dasher out of the ice cream churn and begins licking it.)*

(It has rained. The cake, at least, is safe on the porch.)

LAURA LEE *(cont.)* Ladies, let's don't despair. Now that the sun's out, this yard'll dry right up. All is not lost.

GLENDINE. Except our groom.

BOBRITA. Just a minor component.

(They continue eating dejectedly. They moan with ice cream headaches.)

VIOLET. Ice cream gives me a terrible headache.

BOBRITA. It does everybody, Sister.

GLENDINE. I'm going to run check on our little bride.

LAURA LEE. Don't bother her. She's sound asleep.

(The telephone rings. **LAURA LEE** *jumps on it.)*

Hello...Oh, Laverne! Did you...What?...Laverne, I know you think it's the bus fumes giving you those sick headaches, but have you ever considered it's the Change? Now about...Yes, I'm sure it...Laverne, this is crucial! Did you reach the ticket woman back where he got on the bus?...Well, what'd she say?...

(to the women)

The woman at the other station said there were so many servicemen, she doesn't know if he got on the bus or not.

VIOLET. *(hopefully)* That means he still could have gotten on it.

BOBRITA. Yes, but he didn't get off it.

LAURA LEE. *(on the telephone)* Now listen to me, Laverne. Pay close attention. I want you to track down the bus driver at his next stop. Find out what he says…We'll be forever grateful. Take your powders.

(She hangs up.)

GLENDINE. There must be some explanation. Any boy that would fall in love with a girl in a livestock barn is serious.

VIOLET. And he gave up that Jimmie Sue for her.

BOBRITA. Did you ever think, girls – it's just the age-old story of getting left at the church.

VIOLET. Sister!

BOBRITA. We'd better start calling people, heading them off at the pass.

LAURA LEE. *(strongly)* No! – I mean – that's a little premature, don't you think, Bobrita?

BOBRITA. Am I the only one around here who's not blind?

LAURA LEE. *(firmly)* We're going to wait. At least until we hear from Laverne. He can't have just – disappeared.

(A moment as the women take in **LAURA LEE***'s seriousness.)*

GLENDINE. Well, I guess I'll get those Bluebonnet costumes done or those girls'll be going out there jaybird. Where'd I put my sewing?

LAURA LEE. In the parlor.

GLENDINE. Holler if you hear anything.

*(***GLENDINE*** goes inside.)*

BOBRITA. We didn't take her on to raise, Laura Lee.

VIOLET. Sister, we have to be Good Samaritans and care for the less fortunate.

BOBRITA. Sister, I've been caring for the less fortunate for the last forty years.

VIOLET. Really? What are you implying?

LAURA LEE. Ladies, ladies –

BOBRITA. No implication intended. We built you that little house to move into – that's a pretty strong hint.

(*VIOLET, stung, reaches for the smelling salts.*)

VIOLET. Well, I hope I'm allowed to come back on the property and pick up my pup.

BOBRITA. What pup?

VIOLET. You promised me the runt.

BOBRITA. And where do you think you're going to put him? Not only didn't Glendine bargain on you, she sure didn't plan on raising a suckling pup. I think you've imposed enough without taking on any livestock.

LAURA LEE. All right, Bobrita –

VIOLET. Imposed? What do you mean?

BOBRITA. Sister, how long do you think Glendine and Coach are going to let you camp out on their doorstep?

VIOLET. Where do you suggest I live since you no longer desire my company on the ranch?

BOBRITA. You're the one who piked off. That little house we built you – at considerable expense to the management – you didn't stay in one night.

VIOLET. There was a wolf howling –

BOBRITA. There hasn't been a wolf in this county since the Alamo –

VIOLET. And a bear or a bobcat clawing outside the window –

BOBRITA. You just wanted to get back into your old room in the main house –

VIOLET. And why not? It's my house, too.

BOBRITA. Your house, too?! Based on what? Squatter's rights?

VIOLET. Doesn't forty years count for something?

BOBRITA. It counts for wearing out your welcome! Look, Sister, Beaumont and I are a married couple and Glendine and Coach are a married couple. You're my sister and I promised Daddy-Bob and Mama-Rita I'd look after you, but nobody else is going to.

VIOLET. *(tearing up)* Well, if Glendine feels that way, I'll just make other arrangements. I don't stay where I'm not wanted.

BOBRITA. First I heard tell of it.

(GLENDINE comes out from the house wearing the pep squad costume she's been working on, with its short pleated skirt and sequined bluebonnets.)

GLENDINE. Ta-da!

(The others are aghast.)

BOBRITA. *(after a beat)* Blue never was your color, Glendine.

LAURA LEE. What ever possessed you??

GLENDINE. I didn't have a dress form.

BOBRITA. Did it ever dawn on you there might be a slight change in your figure after forty years?

GLENDINE. What change?

BOBRITA. Tempus does fugit.

VIOLET. You're just a bit more mature is what she means.

GLENDINE. I know what she means. And I'm here to tell you my measurements are the same as when I was in high school.

BOBRITA. The numbers may be the same, but they're in reverse order.

GLENDINE. But don't you think it's cute?

LAURA LEE. After a certain age, cute does not apply.

BOBRITA. Has Coach seen you in this rig?

GLENDINE. Several times! And out of it!

VIOLET. *(putting her hands over her ears)* Glendine!

(IMA JEAN comes out with her suitcase.)

IMA JEAN. 'Scuse me. Y'all have done so much for me and I appreciate it, but I best be on my way.

LAURA LEE. Sweetheart, no! Laverne's contacting the bus driver. He'll clear all this up. Jesse's going to walk through that door, I know it! I know he will!

IMA JEAN. No, Miss Laura Lee. I don't mean to backtalk you, but this isn't the first time I've been abandoned. I know the signs.

LAURA LEE. You can't give up yet, precious! You can't! He's going to come!

*(She casts about, looking for something to distract **IMA JEAN**.)*

Why, here we're all sitting like birds in the wilderness when I can predict the outcome of this. Astrology! Before our very eyes!

(She pulls down the chart at her desk.)

Ima Jean, sweetheart, come sit here beside me. That's right. Now, all I need to know is yours and Jesse's birthdays and I can determine your destiny.

BOBRITA. That's an awful big assignment.

LAURA LEE. *(getting out her astrology books and a big chief tablet)* All right, what month and day were you born?

IMA JEAN. September the eighteenth.

LAURA LEE. And Jesse?

IMA JEAN. January the third.

LAURA LEE. Ahhhhhh! This is the meeting of the Virgin and the Goat! Interesting that you two should be paired –

(consulting her books)

– because of your strong compatibility –

(thumbing through)

– and your equally strong incompatibility.

BOBRITA. Well, that clears everything up.

LAURA LEE. *(reading to **IMA JEAN**)* You're modest and shy. You represent purity and perfection. You may find a career in fashion for you have a flair for dress.

BOBRITA. Come again?

LAURA LEE. *(another passage)* Now, your Capricorn is the most determined and persistent sign of the Zodiac. He's a down-to-earth realist and willing to take care of the daily chores.

GLENDINE. That means you won't have to worry about feeding the goats.

LAURA LEE. He's a trustworthy and loyal person. Once he commits to something, he unfailingly sees it through to the end.

VIOLET. See! That's proof positive he'll be here.

LAURA LEE. Yes, that's right!!

(another passage)

Now, Capricorns are also prone to – uh-oh, here's something else you have in common – stomach and bowel upsets.

BOBRITA. Better watch out for the Mexican food in Galveston.

GLENDINE. Laura Lee, leave out the unromantic parts.

LAURA LEE. *(making a pronouncement)* With their shared values of hard work and attention to detail, this couple will have a life of domestic and romantic bliss. If a perfect match existed, this would be it!

GLENDINE. Oh! I knew it!

LAURA LEE. *(pulling out another book)* Now it wouldn't surprise me if that Jimmie Sue's a Scorpio –

(The telephone rings.)

Hello…Yes…Oh…

(crestfallen)

Oh, I see…Well, thank you for calling, Laverne.

(She hangs up.)

GLENDINE. What'd she say?

LAURA LEE. The bus driver did a head count at every stop. Nobody was missing the whole trip. Said if Jesse didn't get off the bus, that means he was never on it.

(A long beat.)

IMA JEAN. Well, I guess I'll leave on the 9:30 bus.

*(**LAURA LEE** sinks onto the porch steps.)*

GLENDINE. *(to* **IMA JEAN***)* Now, he's not the only man in the world, precious. My philosophy has always been if you miss the bus, there's another one right behind it.

IMA JEAN. I'll just go inside and wash my face and get my things.

(She goes inside.)

LAURA LEE. *(to herself)* Just disappeared –

BOBRITA. We better go down to the square and send out the word to cancel. While we're at it, Laura Lee, we'll help you load up some of these papers and junk and dump them off.

VIOLET. I stopped by the Air Raid Warden's office while I was down on the square. They need everything they can get.

GLENDINE. I'll gather up the Ladies Home Companions.

BOBRITA. Violet, you tote all the Readers Digests. Unless you're just too fragile in this heat.

VIOLET. *(her hackles up)* I believe I can handle it with the help of the Lord.

LAURA LEE. *(snapping back)* Now, hold your horses a minute. This is my job and I'll get to it.

BOBRITA. Yes, but when?

LAURA LEE. I don't need any prodding from you, Bobrita. Now, let's get back to our meeting, get some things settled.

BOBRITA. *(setting down her stack of papers)* Fine. Let's make it quick.

*(***LAURA LEE*** leads them to the meeting table.)*

GLENDINE. I think we should sell souvenirs. We can make candy. I have all kinds of molds – stars, Uncle Sam –

BOBRITA. That's an expense we don't need.

VIOLET. First we have to call the meeting to order again.

BOBRITA. I move we dispense with Robert's Rules of Order.

GLENDINE. Second.

LAURA LEE. So moved.

VIOLET. But –

LAURA LEE. Sit down, Violet.

VIOLET. You are all out of order.

GLENDINE. Once again, I propose a talent show.

BOBRITA. Aren't we putting the cart before the horse? We haven't even decided if we're having the Gala here –

LAURA LEE. If we're going to have the Gala here? It's decided and it's going to stay decided. Now I think we should have a fashion show. That should shake some money loose from the men in the crowd.

BOBRITA. At our age, a fashion show is ridiculous.

GLENDINE. Speak for yourself.

BOBRITA. I say we get all the shops in the square to contribute something. Have a silent auction –

GLENDINE. Your husband owns all that property on the square. They're all your renters. Don't you think that's extortion?

BOBRITA. Do you want this Gala to be a success or not?

VIOLET. My cookbook would sell. It isn't just recipes. You get Bible verses and rules to live by. We can all contribute –

LAURA LEE. Bobrita can't cook, Glendine eats down at the country club, and I don't give my recipes out.

GLENDINE. I know, I know! We could have a raffle.

LAURA LEE. That's next door to gambling.

BOBRITA. Naturally you'd think of that because you lived in Nevada. Getting that divorce. Whichever one it was.

GLENDINE. I'd like to know who declared it open season on Glendine.

BOBRITA. You're a pretty easy target to hit.

GLENDINE. Oh, I see. Beware the green-eyed monster. This goes all the way back to high school. It's not my fault I was elected Football Queen and Basketball Queen both.

BOBRITA. And here you are running around with the pep squad again.

LAURA LEE. If you'll recall, it's been ever since high school we've been coming to your defense.

GLENDINE. Coming to my defense??

VIOLET. It breaks our hearts when people gossip about you.

GLENDINE. I beg your pardon!

BOBRITA. The twins claim it's you and Coach who need a chaperone in the back seat of the bus going to the Away games.

GLENDINE. Me and Coach?! He's my husband! And I'm just having fun!

LAURA LEE. Well, you've sure had plenty – husbands AND fun!

VIOLET. Now, girls, Glendine needs our help, not our criticism.

GLENDINE. *(to* **VIOLET***, indignant)* Your help?! What help can you give me? You've never stood on your own two feet. You've always been taken care of.

VIOLET. You know good and well my health has prevented me from doing too much.

GLENDINE. I've never been to Doctor McGreevey's office in my life as much as I've been the last three weeks. There was the time she flipped out of the hammock and got the wind knocked out of her –

VIOLET. I thought I cracked a rib –

GLENDINE. And the time in the middle of the night when she stepped on her bridgework –

VIOLET. There was no night light –

BOBRITA. She's not running a bed and board.

GLENDINE. And the time her heart was racing and I found out later it was because she'd run into Coach in the hall in his undershorts.

VIOLET. He should have had on a robe.

LAURA LEE. It's his house!

BOBRITA. Sister, you've been exposed. You've hollered wolf too many times.

(to **GLENDINE**)

You'll notice she hollers louder whenever there's work to be done.

LAURA LEE. Some people are like the lilies of the field. They neither toil nor spin.

VIOLET. I beg your pardon.

LAURA LEE. My brother always said when he married Bobrita, he married Violet, too.

BOBRITA. I beg your pardon.

LAURA LEE. Well, you and Violet have traveled in lockstep your whole lives.

BOBRITA. Not so! She's tagged along!

LAURA LEE. You've allowed it.

BOBRITA. How do you get that?

LAURA LEE. If you didn't have Violet, you wouldn't have anybody to boss around –

VIOLET. Amen!

LAURA LEE. – because Beaumont sure won't put up with it. He's endured Violet living there all these years so you'd have somebody to lord it over.

GLENDINE. Poor Beaumont.

BOBRITA & VIOLET. (together) Poor Beaumont?!

LAURA LEE. You two girls have always taken Beaumont for granted. When he's been nothing but kind-hearted and sympathetic. If Beaumont hadn't come along, you'd still be clerking at the feed store.

BOBRITA. Yes, that's right. Unlike you, Laura Lee, I know what it's like to pull myself up and make my own way in the world. I don't mind admitting I started out like a runt gnawing on the hind tit.

LAURA LEE. Must you be so blunt? I've made my own way in the world just the same as you! And gone on to serve this town as the Mayor's wife for thirty-five years! But I was always taught there's a right way and a wrong way to –

BOBRITA. *(bristling)* To what?

LAURA LEE. To get things done –

BOBRITA. Get things done??

> *(a sweeping gesture at the porch and yard)*

What would you know about getting things done? This running around of yours – spinning your wheels doing everything except what needs to get done – just makes more work for the rest of us.

> *(**IMA JEAN** has come out onto the porch with her suitcase, unseen.)*

LAURA LEE. There are a great many people who depend on me. I have many responsibilities I can't neglect.

BOBRITA. Your responsibility is here at home. That's what you're neglecting.

VIOLET. We've tried to help you, but you won't let us.

BOBRITA. We're giving you an ultimatum here and now, Laura Lee. Either you get this yard in order or I'll give the Gala.

GLENDINE. I second the motion!

LAURA LEE. I find it very hard to take you seriously, Glendine, when you're rigged out in that ensemble.

> *(The argument starts to overlap as it grows more heated.)*

GLENDINE. Laura Lee, please don't take on my appearance as another one of your projects –

VIOLET. It's high time somebody did.

GLENDINE. May I remind you you're currently dependent on my largesse –

VIOLET. I thought you and Coach enjoyed my companionship –

BOBRITA. You might want to rethink that –

VIOLET. Well! I guess my picture's been turned toward the wall.

GLENDINE. And your high-handedness, Bobrita, goes all the way back to when we were Campfire Girls. You've always had more nerve than a tooth.

LAURA LEE. This from the Campfire Girl who raised money by selling kisses instead of cookies –

GLENDINE. We should sell kisses for the Gala!

LAURA LEE. Not at my house you won't. It's a good thing I know how to give a –

VIOLET. You may know how, Laura Lee, but the question is when –

BOBRITA. I just thank the Lord that boy of Ima Jean's didn't show up today. I'd be ashamed for people to see the state of –

LAURA LEE. Ashamed?!!

BOBRITA. Ashamed! You run around town, involve yourself in everybody else's lives, think you can run the show and not answer to anybody just because you're the Mayor's wife. Well, you're not the Mayor's wife anymore.

(A long beat.)

(Wounded, **LAURA LEE** *turns to go inside. She sees* **IMA JEAN** *on the porch.)*

IMA JEAN. I've got to get on back to Gillette. I'll see tomorrow if I can't get me a job clerking at Liggett's. I'm on my own now. Back at the orphanage, I was one of many, many, many. Nobody paid no attention to me. I've always been like a piece of torn newspaper caught on a barbed-wire fence, blowing lonesome in the wind. But then you run onto me today and took me up. And I'll be forever grateful. To all of you. Miss Laura Lee, you all don't know how lucky you are to have each other.

(She takes up her valise and goes into the house. A beat, then we hear the front door open and close.)

(The telephone rings. **LAURA LEE** *answers it.)*

LAURA LEE. Hello…

(simply, holding out the telephone)

It's Jesse.

(The women run for the telephone. **BOBRITA** *grabs it.)*

(As they pass the telephone around, **LAURA LEE** *slips inside.)*

BOBRITA. *(on the telephone)* Young man, this is Mrs. Beaumont Tolliver. I demand to know where you've been. You've had us worried sick.

GLENDINE. *(grabbing the telephone)* I hear you're a redhead! I can't wait to meet you – I'm partial to redheads!

VIOLET. *(taking it)* You are the prodigal son returned!

BOBRITA. *(getting it back)* I believe you owe us an explanation, son, and it better be a good one...You what?

(reporting)

He decided to hitch-hike. Figured he'd beat the bus and surprise Ima Jean –

*(***GLENDINE** *takes the telephone away from* **BOBRITA.***)*

GLENDINE. *(on the telephone, to Jesse)* Sweetheart, what held you up?

VIOLET. *(grabbing it)* Who brought you into town?

BOBRITA. *(grabbing the telephone back)* Put Laverne on the telephone.

(taking the telephone)

Laverne! Throw a rope around that boy and hold him there. Buy him a Dr. Pepper. Don't let him out of your sight. Then at six-thirty, send him down here.

(She hangs up. The women squeal in delight.)

GLENDINE. We've got a groom!

VIOLET. We've got a wedding!

(calling upstairs)

Laura Lee, the wedding's on!

BOBRITA. I knew all along he'd show up.

(A beat. then they realize:)

GLENDINE. Ima Jean!

VIOLET. Now we've lost the bride again!

GLENDINE. I'll run after her.

BOBRITA. She can't be more than half a block.

VIOLET. Hurry!

(**GLENDINE** *runs out.*)

BOBRITA. She'll stop traffic in that get-up.

(**BOBRITA** *starts straightening up the porch, spreading and smoothing quilts.* **VIOLET** *approaches.*)

VIOLET. Sister – let me help you –

(working her courage up)

– I've been noticing, Sister – down at the square – this sign. At the Air Raid Warden's office. Says "Assistant Wanted." They need somebody to organize the household contributions for the war effort.

(as they cover the stacks of papers and magazines)

Like all this – I'm going to apply for that job.

BOBRITA. You're going to what?

VIOLET. Apply for the job.

BOBRITA. Oh now, Sister –

VIOLET. I need to stand on my own two feet.

BOBRITA. Sister, how does it feel to lose your mind? Now it's time for you to leave Glendine's and come back home.

VIOLET. No! I don't intend to impose on Glendine – or you – anymore. I'm going to live on my own.

BOBRITA. What??

*(It starts to dawn on **BOBRITA** that **VIOLET** is in earnest.)*

Where do you think you're going to live?

VIOLET. I'll be fine. Don't worry about me.

BOBRITA. Don't worry about you? You've been my responsibility ever since Daddy-Bob and Mama-Rita have been gone.

VIOLET. But I don't want to be your responsibility any more.

BOBRITA. But Sister – Now, you don't have to move back into the cabin. You just come back into the main house. Into your old room. I'll tell Beaumont you –

VIOLET. Sister – no – my mind's made up.

BOBRITA. But – but – but you've been gone long enough.

(A beat, then she comes as close as she can to admitting it herself.)

Besides, Sister – the dogs need you.

VIOLET. There is one thing you can do for me.

BOBRITA. What?

VIOLET. There's an apartment above the War Bond office. You and Beaumont own that building. Let me rent it from you.

BOBRITA. Oh, Sister, I'll just let you have it.

VIOLET. No, I'm going to pay my own way.

BOBRITA. How are you going to afford rent on that little salary?

VIOLET. – I don't know – I'll cut back –

BOBRITA. But you get so scared by yourself –

VIOLET. *(starting to lose her nerve a little)* – well – when my pup is grown, he'll protect me –

BOBRITA. – Are you sure, Sister?

VIOLET. *(resolved)* Just as sure as I am that the gates are pearly.

GLENDINE. *(from inside)* I've got her!

VIOLET. Eureka!

(GLENDINE runs on with IMA JEAN. They are both flushed with excitement.)

Isn't it wonderful, honey!

IMA JEAN. Oh, yes, ma'am!

BOBRITA. See how all your doubts and fears were unfounded? I knew it all along.

GLENDINE. Bobrita, you run get the tablecloths and I'll get the plates –

VIOLET. *(hopping to it)* I'll lay out the silverware. Glendine, you bring out the –

*(**LAURA LEE** comes out onto the porch. She is carrying her wedding dress. The others stop in their tracks.)*

Laura Lee!

*(**LAURA LEE** comes down to **IMA JEAN** on the porch steps.)*

LAURA LEE. *(to **IMA JEAN**)* Sweetheart, if I say so myself, I was a beautiful bride. But I've kept this dress locked away. To protect it. And myself. When you remember the beginning of something, it forces you to remember the end. When the volunteers were so long coming back from Matagorda and R.L. wasn't with them, I thought he'd just gotten lost – gotten separated from them and would of course return soon. So I kept myself busy, ran around all day so I wouldn't think about him all night. But, you know, the heart has a mind of its own. It can be so willful.

(She turns to the women.)

Ladies, I've made a decision about the Gala. It should be a tribute to R.L. R.L. believed in this town since it was nothing but a feed store and a hitching post. The way to honor him is for people to talk about him, to share their memories of him and to give to the war effort in his name – Robert Lee McInerny.

*(She gives **IMA JEAN** her wedding dress.)*

Sweetheart, I hope this dress brings you as many years of happiness as it did me.

IMA JEAN. Oh, Miss Laura Lee – thank you.

LAURA LEE. No, sweetheart. Thank you. – Now run upstairs, quick. Jesse's on his way.

*(**IMA JEAN** runs inside.)*

*(**LAURA LEE** turns to the misty-eyed women.)*

LAURA LEE *(cont.)* *(clapping her hands)* What are we waiting for? I can't do all this by myself. I need your help.

(They rush around doing a myriad of tasks in a few minutes – pruning, putting away garden tools, hanging bunting, laying out linens, china, and silver.)

(Overcoming their differences, they are a well-choreographed team, working together to spectacular effect.)

(They try to spruce up the yard, but the planters look woefully short on flowers. **LAURA LEE** *hits on a genius idea – she grabs some mason jars from a pile on the porch and sticks some cut flowers from the buckets into the jars. The women bury the mason jars in the planters and, voila, instant springtime.)*

(As the others keep working in the garden, **GLENDINE** *piles herself high with wedding dress after wedding dress from the porch and runs inside with them. After a bit, she returns – she has changed out of the bluebonnet costume and back into her playset, with the skirt demurely buttoned down the front.)*

(She has the hatboxes from the square stacked in her arms.)

GLENDINE. Catch, girls!

(She tosses hats to the ladies from the porch.)

BOBRITA. Don't you look swell.

GLENDINE. *(with a glance at her outfit)* Well, I've covered up my best features – but I thought this was more appropriate.

(As they put the finishing touches on the yard, **IMA JEAN** *comes out in* **LAURA LEE***'s wedding dress.)*

(She is holding the shoes and veil. The dress is undone in back.)

IMA JEAN. *(reaching around)* – these little bitty buttons –

*(***GLENDINE** *and* **VIOLET** *get her into her shoes and veil as* **LAURA LEE** *and* **BOBRITA** *work on the buttons.)*

GLENDINE. Girls, we almost forgot! Our something old, something new, something borrowed, something blue!

LAURA LEE. Oh! Well, my dress is certainly old.

BOBRITA. Then something new.

VIOLET. The New Testament is new!

(She races to her purse and pulls out her little white New Testament.)

GLENDINE. No, Violet, let your New Testament be something borrowed. I've got something new.

(She runs to her packages from her little shopping trip on the square. She pulls out a garter.)

Ooh-la-la, precious!

(She holds up a silky nightgown trimmed in lace.)

And I couldn't resist this. Perfect for your honeymoon!

(IMA JEAN ducks her chin in embarrassment.)

IMA JEAN. Thank you, Miss Glendine.

LAURA LEE. Now, something blue.

VIOLET. *(thinking)* Something blue –

BOBRITA. *(scanning the yard)* What's blue?

GLENDINE. *(searching)* Blue –

(Finally –)

BOBRITA. I've got it. Is Jesse a hunting man?

IMA JEAN. Yes, ma'am.

BOBRITA. Then I'll send you my best blue-tick pup.

IMA JEAN. Oh, thank you! He'll love it.

(The doorbell rings. The women hurriedly take off their aprons.)

LAURA LEE. Sweetheart, he can't see you before the wedding.

BOBRITA. We've got to get you upstairs.

LAURA LEE. *(stopping short)* Wait! We've never decided the order of your attendants.

GLENDINE. Who's going to be your matron of honor, precious?

VIOLET. Or maid of honor?

IMA JEAN. Well –

(She looks at each of the four women, thinking hard.)

(as she pulls down her veil) – I expect I'm the only bride ever to have three matrons of honor and a maid of honor.

(The women embrace **IMA JEAN**, *then turn to go into the house.)*

BOBRITA. Sister, how much of "O Promise Me" are you going to sing?

VIOLET. All three verses.

LAURA LEE. I hope I made enough punch. As hot as it is –

BOBRITA. All three verses?!

VIOLET. Why certainly! I can't leave out the part about –

GLENDINE. You've got a flat of strawberries. Should we drop them in there, make it go further?

LAURA LEE. We don't have time to wash the sand out of a bunch of strawberries.

BOBRITA. Besides, we're serving peach ice cream –

LAURA LEE. We ate it!!

(By now, the women have disappeared into the house, ready to receive Jesse and all of Eufala Springs.)

(THE CURTAIN FALLS)

(For the curtain call, some companies may wish to continue the story. As the ladies bow, **JESSE** *comes through the door behind them in his infantry uniform, carrying a duffel bag. They turn and see him, and* **IMA JEAN** *runs into his arms. They go into the house arm in arm, followed by the others.)*

(If this choice is followed, the lines describing **JESSE** *in act 1 scene 3 may need to be altered.])*

PROPS

SET DRESSING
Porch: Stacks of magazines and newspapers
Porch: Mason jars (in boxes)
Porch: Miscellaneous recyclable materials, e.g. small scrap metal, cardboard packaging, etc.
Porch: Telephone
Flower pots and planters with overgrown/dried-up flowers
Water bucket under rainspout

FURNITURE
Desk
Chair
Long serving table
Upright piano
Outdoor table and four chairs

FLOWER VARIETIES
Planters and beds: Sweet William
Planters and beds: Hypatia
Planters and beds: Rambling roses

FLOWERS IN BUCKETS
Martha Washington roses
Snapdragons
Bleeding hearts in hanging baskets
Magnolia leaves/branches
Other miscellaneous flowers to fill four to eight buckets

PERSONAL PROPS
Notebook with minutes
Glass of lemonade
Plate with chicken (two legs and a pulley)
Washcloths
Smelling salts
Sewing bag with equipment and big piece of blue satin
Quilts (4 to 6 including wedding ring pattern)
Suitcase
Rag curlers
Hatboxes with hats (4 to 6)
Ice cream churn
Rock salt
Ice
Stack of buffet plates
Silverware
Iced sheet cake
Table linens
4 bowls of ice cream with spoons
Astrology charts, books, writing tablet, pen/pencil
Bunting
White New Testament
Wedding dresses (4 to 6)
Bouquets for curtain call

Additional Titles by
Alan Bailey...

Sanders Family Christmas

**Written by Connie Ray, conceived by Alan Bailey.
Musical Arrangements by John Foley and Gary Fagin.**

Smoke on the Mountain

**Book by Connie Ray, conceived by Alan Bailey.
Musical arrangements by Mike Craver and Mark Hardwick.**

Smoke on the
Mountain Homecoming

**Written by Connie Ray, conceived by Alan Bailey.
Musical arrangements by Mike Craver and Mark Hardwick.**

Please visit our website **samuelfrench.com** for complete
descriptions and licensing information